KING
ARTHUR
and the
Round Table

TALES OF KING ARTHUR

KING ARTHUR
and the
Round Table

written and illustrated by
HUDSON TALBOTT

Books of Wonder Morrow Junior Books New York

Watercolors were used for the full-color illustrations.
The text type is 15-point Goudy Old Style.

Printed in Singapore at Tien Wah Press.
2   3   4   5   6   7   8   9   10

Library of Congress Cataloging-in-Publication Data
Talbott, Hudson.   King Arthur and the Round Table/written and illustrated by Hudson Talbott.
p.   cm.—(Books of wonder) (Tales of King Arthur)
Summary: Retells the story of how the young Arthur became High King of all Britain
and assembled his Knights of the Round Table.
ISBN 0-688-11340-0 (trade)—ISBN 0-688-11341-9 (library)
1. Arthurian romances—Adaptations.   [1. Arthur, King.   2. Folklore—England.   3. Knights and
knighthood—Fiction.]   I. Title.   II. Series.   III. Series: Talbott, Hudson. Tales of King Arthur.
PZ8.1.T133Ki   1995   398.2'094202—dc20   94-43766   CIP   AC

In memory of Mark Darby

Arthur was a lad of only sixteen years when, chosen by adventure and by grace, he became High King of all Britain. But the crown had barely touched his head when trouble broke out. Twelve of the lesser kings refused to accept this unknown country boy as their leader. Jealous and angry at not being chosen themselves, they declared war on their new overlord.

The hostile kings gathered their armies in the fields near Caerleon, Arthur's capital. King Lot, the leader of the rebellion, hoped that the mighty display of men and arms would frighten the untried youth into yielding without a fight. But Arthur had other plans.

Spurring his mount into a frenzied charge, Arthur shot across the field and plunged headlong through the enemy line. His great Pendragon sword blazed around him like a bolt of lightning as he cut his way through the heart of Lot's army. Arthur's knights struggled to match their young king's fury and soon found the enemy scattering before them. By the end of the day, the rebel forces were in disarray, and Arthur claimed his first major victory.

But the rebellion continued. For months the warring parties chased and fought each other all over Britain. The shifting patterns of advance and retreat, victory and defeat, continued relentlessly until Arthur could no longer stand to see his fellow Britons killing one another. He asked his counselor, Merlin, to help him devise a plan that would bring this civil war to an end.

Merlin went to France and made alliances with King Ban and King Bors and returned to Britain with their armies. Hiding them in the dense forest of Bedegraine, he instructed Arthur to lure Lot's army into the valley nearby.

As Arthur and his men turned to face the enemy, the surrounding forest suddenly exploded with the deafening war cries of his allies. Lot's soldiers faltered, crashing together in panic, when they saw the colors of King Ban and King Bors flooding down the hillsides.

By dusk hundreds lay dead, yet the combat raged on. Although the ambush had given Arthur an early advantage, Lot's greater numbers were now overwhelming him. Then Arthur saw a chance of turning the tide. Noticing that Lot was meeting with the other rebel kings away from their armies, Arthur and his knights rushed forth, blocking their return to the battlefield. Leaderless and exhausted, the enemy soldiers soon broke ranks and fled into the night.

The next morning Arthur wandered through the battlefield alone to see for himself what his victory had cost in human
life. Once-glorious knights and humble foot soldiers, old friends
and sworn enemies—all lay together now.

In the distance, a maiden was helping the nuns care for
the wounded. The sunlight shimmering in her hair reminded
Arthur of his last golden summer before he was crowned king,
before the wars. His heart touched, he picked a wild rose and
quietly approached the girl.

"Young soldier," she called. "Let me see to that wound."

Arthur hadn't noticed the small gash on his forehead. He knelt beside the girl, and she set to work cleaning and dressing his injury.

"Are you a nun?" asked Arthur.

"No. I'm studying the healing arts with the holy sisters. Now hold still," she said, wrapping a cloth around his head.

Arthur silently obeyed. Female hands were so *gentle*, he noticed, so *comforting*. Shyly, he held out the rose.

"For me?" asked the girl, a bit surprised by the offering.

Arthur nodded. She smiled and held the flower to her nose.

"A perfect blossom," she said, gazing down at it, "even in all this ruin."

"Like you," Arthur blurted, flushing bright red.

"Pardon?" she asked, suddenly looking up. As the nuns' cart began to move away, she stood up to follow it.

"May I call upon you?" asked Arthur.

The girl stopped and looked back at him, then slowly smiled. "If only that were possible," she replied sadly. "Our convent was burned, and I must return home. Besides, you'll probably be in another battle by nightfall. But thank you for the rose. It shall always remind me of the lad I met at Bedegraine." With that, she leaned forward and kissed him on the cheek, then ran to join her companions.

Arthur stood and watched the girl disappear in the distance, then slowly touched his cheek where she had kissed it.

In the months following the hard-won triumph at Bedegraine, Arthur's fame spread throughout Britain. Many admirers came to Caerleon, offering their services to the daring young hero. But Arthur could think only of the girl. For hours he would sit, gazing out the window.

"Your Majesty?" implored Merlin. "Your Grace?... ARTHUR!"

Arthur looked up from his reverie.

"You must forget that girl!" scolded the frustrated wizard. "Someday we will consider the proper alliance for your marriage, but we have much to do before then. Look at your court! Grown men, many of them kings in their own lands, fighting like children over places at your table! They're not used to working together. You have to show them leadership, Arthur, or you'll never hold their loyalty."

Arthur sank back in his seat and stared at the floor, stung by the truth of Merlin's words. "How can I be a leader to men twice my age?" he sighed. "Some of them have *grandsons* older than me! It was so much simpler leading them in battle than governing them in peace."

"Fighting is always simpler than seeking a means of preventing it," said Merlin. "Yet the fighting among your men is no different from wars between nations. A great leader finds a way to make peace while bringing honor and respect to everyone.

"Trust yourself, lad," he added. "It is no accident that you wear the crown."

"If only I knew how," Arthur mumbled pensively. "If only I could show them that by honoring one another, we honor ourselves."

His thoughts were interrupted by a messenger from King Ryence. The savage old warrior-king of North Wales was notorious for decorating his cloak with the beards of kings he had conquered, and now he wanted Arthur's. This amused Merlin greatly, for Arthur still could not grow a beard.

But the laughing stopped when the messenger told them that Ryence had already attacked the neighboring kingdom of Cameliard, home of Arthur's ally King Leodegrance.

Cameliard had been under siege for many days by the time
Arthur and his knights arrived. Not having had time to raise a
large force, Arthur could only hope to affect the outcome by
confronting Ryence himself.

Arthur and his men charged madly through the enemy camp, cutting a path toward King Ryence. Surprised by Arthur's burst of fury, the old warrior scrambled to retreat, but Arthur pursued him across the littered field. The enemy soldiers quickly scattered when they saw their leader fleeing.

From the castle towers, Leodegrance's knights saw Arthur's bold performance and were inspired to join him. Together they chased the retreating enemy troops deep into the hills of North Wales.

As Arthur returned to Cameliard, his weary spirits were lifted by the cheering crowds that awaited him. Merlin, however, was more concerned with the business at hand.

"Leodegrance will probably offer you anything you want as a reward, including his daughter's hand in marriage. But the stars do not bode well for this union."

"You needn't worry, Merlin," said Arthur. "My people are my only concern now."

"Well then, you'll be pleased to know that Leodegrance possesses an object of far greater value to you," continued Merlin, "an object of great power and mystery that I created for your father, Uther-Pendragon, long ago—"

Merlin stopped abruptly as King Leodegrance stepped forward to greet them. He ushered his guests into his castle and called for his daughter to attend them.

"Your Majesty, this is Guinevere. She is—" The king stopped short as Arthur rushed past him toward the girl.

"She is everything to me," said Arthur. "Ever since that morning at Bedegraine I've dreamt of this moment. My dear Lady Guinevere, will you marry me?"

"Yes, my lord," she said, taking his hands in hers, "with all my heart."

King Leodegrance laughed with delight at having his secret wish fulfilled so quickly. But Merlin smiled sadly, for he knew more of the future than he wished to know.

Insisting on showing his wedding present to the young couple immediately, King Leodegrance led them down dark corridors to an ancient banquet hall. There, in the dim light, Arthur's eyes fell upon an enormous wooden disk, decorated with the sun and moon and all the signs of the zodiac.

"Your father asked me to safeguard this table until his rightful heir should appear," said King Leodegrance. "May it serve you and my daughter well."

With the wondrous object now in Arthur's possession, Merlin breathed a sigh of relief. Guinevere kissed and thanked her father. But Arthur stood motionless, staring at the huge disk.

"This is it, Merlin," Arthur whispered. "This will be my hub. We'll gather round this table as equals. Like spokes of a great wheel, the light of Truth shall radiate out through our brotherhood, to touch all who long for justice, honor, and mercy." He paused and turned to Guinevere. "My lady, I want to create a home for us and a fitting hall for this great table—a place where dreams and ideas can come to life. I need your help to fulfill this vision."

"Of course, Arthur," she replied. "It is *our* vision now."

Arthur turned and embraced Leodegrance. "Thank you, my friend," he said, "on behalf of myself, my father, and the people of Britain."

With Merlin's magical assistance, a spectacular palace swiftly rose upon enchanted meadows where the ancient fairy folk once abided. In their honor Arthur named his home as the Old Ones had called their domain, Camelot.

Meanwhile, word spread throughout the world that the new High King of all Britain was assembling an extraordinary court. From near and far, knights and nobles rode forth to Camelot, hoping to prove themselves worthy of this splendid new company.

Finally, the great palace was completed, and Arthur's beloved Lady Guinevere arrived for their long-awaited wedding day.

Following the ceremony, Arthur and Guinevere led their guests to the Hall of the Round Table. When all were assembled, Arthur bade Merlin call forth those knights whom he had chosen for his new order of knighthood. As the old enchanter called out the name of each knight, that name magically appeared on the back of the seat reserved for him. The final place, called the Siege Perilous, was left empty, reserved for the purest knight who would one day come to Camelot.

With the fellowship now seated, Merlin drew the knights' attention upward, above the table. Calling upon his mystical powers, he conjured visions of their glorious future and the heroes who would soon join them.

Arthur then stood and led the knights in an oath of loyalty to their cause.

"We rise now and lift our swords as the Knights of the Round Table. May these blades work together as a single force to protect the innocent, defend the weak, and free the oppressed. May the bond of our brotherhood inspire our service to humanity, and may the deeds of each bring honor to us all."

AFTERWORD

The tales of King Arthur and the Knights of the Round Table are some of the most popular stories in the English language. Ever since the nineteenth century, they have been perennial favorites with young readers and listeners around the world.

These legends, however, date back over a thousand years and were originally told among adults as entertainment and history. Books about the adventures of King Arthur and his knights can be found as far back as the fifteenth century. In fact, King Arthur was the subject of one of the first books ever printed in England—Sir Thomas Malory's *Morte Darthur*. Published in 1485 by the great English printer William Caxton, this book is considered by many to be the definitive work about Arthur and his knights.

But like so many other great old stories, the legends of King Arthur were told and retold by many different people for hundreds of years before they were ever put down in the pages of a book. No one person can be credited with the many legends of the Round Table, and each generation finds new meaning and crafts new stories from these myths.

In creating a series of storybooks based on the tales of King Arthur, Hudson Talbott has immersed himself in the history of Arthur and crafted a work rich in the chivalry and romance of the legends yet filled with timeless themes. In his young Arthur we see the struggles of any caring leader to unite his people and lead them to a brighter future. And in his Camelot we see a home for the dreams and hopes of people from around the world.

—*Peter Glassman*